THE
EYE OF
APOLLO

G.K. Chesterton

first published in

1911

That singular smoky sparkle, at once a confusion and a transparency, which is the strange secret of the Thames, was changing more and more from its grey to its glittering extreme as the sun climbed to the zenith over Westminster, and two men crossed Westminster Bridge. One man was very tall and the other very short; they might even have been fantastically compared to the arrogant clock-tower of Parliament and the humbler humped shoulders of the Abbey, for the short man was in clerical dress. The official description of the tall man was M. Hercule Flambeau, private detective, and he was going to his new offices in a new pile of flats facing the Abbey entrance. The official description of the short man was the Reverend J. Brown, attached to St. Francis Xavier's Church, Camberwell, and he was coming from a Camberwell deathbed to see the new offices of his friend.

The building was

American in its sky-scraping altitude, and American also in the oiled elaboration of its machinery of telephones and lifts. But it was barely finished and still understaffed; only three tenants had moved in; the office just above Flambeau was occupied, as also was the office just below him; the two floors above that and the three floors below were entirely bare. But the first glance at the new tower of flats caught something much more arresting. Save for a few relics of scaffolding, the one glaring object was erected outside the office just above Flambeau's. It was an enormous gilt effigy of the human eye, surrounded with rays of gold, and taking up as much room as two or three of the office windows.

"What on earth is that?" asked Father Brown, and stood still. "Oh, a new religion," said Flambeau, laughing; "one of those new religions that forgive your sins by saying you never had any. Rather like Christian

Science, I should think. The fact is that a fellow calling himself Kalon (I don't know what his name is, except that it can't be that) has taken the flat just above me. I have two lady typewriters underneath me, and this enthusiastic old humbug on top. He calls himself the New Priest of Apollo, and he worships the sun."

"Let him look out," said Father Brown. "The sun was the cruellest of all the gods. But what does that monstrous eye mean?"

"As I understand it, it is a theory of theirs," answered Flambeau, "that a man can endure anything if his mind is quite steady. Their two great symbols are the sun and the open eye; for they say that if a man were really healthy he could stare at the sun."

"If a man were really healthy," said Father Brown, "he would not bother to stare at it."

"Well, that's all I can tell you about the new religion," went on Flambeau carelessly. "It claims, of course, that it can cure all physical diseases."

"Can it cure the one spiritual disease?" asked Father Brown, with a serious curiosity.

"And what is the one spiritual disease?" asked Flambeau, smiling.

"Oh, thinking one is quite well," said his friend.

Flambeau was more interested in the quiet little office below him than in the flamboyant temple above. He was a lucid Southerner, incapable of conceiving himself as anything but a Catholic or an atheist; and new religions of a bright and pallid sort were not much in his line. But humanity was always in his line, especially when it was good-looking; moreover, the ladies downstairs were characters in their way. The office was kept by two sisters, both slight and dark, one of them tall and striking. She had a dark, eager and aquiline profile, and was one of those women whom one always thinks of in profile, as of the clean-cut edge of some weapon. She seemed to cleave her way through life. She had eyes of startling brilliancy, but it was the brilliancy of steel rather than of diamonds; and her straight, slim figure was a shade too stiff for its grace. Her younger sister was like her shortened shadow, a little greyer, paler, and more insignificant.

They both wore a business-like black, with little masculine cuffs and collars. There are thousands of such curt, strenuous ladies in the offices of London, but the interest of these lay rather in their real than their apparent position.

For Pauline Stacey, the elder, was

actually the heiress of a crest and half a county, as well as great wealth; she had been brought up in castles and gardens, before a frigid fierceness (peculiar to the modern woman) had driven her to what she considered a harsher and a higher existence. She had not, indeed, surrendered her money; in that there would have been a romantic or monkish abandon quite alien to her masterful utilitarianism. She held her wealth, she would say, for use upon practical social objects. Part of it she had put into her business, the nucleus of a model typewriting emporium; part of it was distributed

in various leagues
and causes for the
advancement of
such work among
women. How far
Joan, her sister
and partner, shared
this slightly prosaic
idealism no one
could be very sure.
But she followed
her leader with a
dog-like affection
which was somehow
more attractive, with
its touch of tragedy,

than the hard, high spirits of the elder. For Pauline Stacey had nothing to say to tragedy; she was understood to deny its existence.

Her rigid rapidity and cold impatience had amused Flambeau very much on the first occasion of his entering the flats. He had lingered outside the lift in the entrance hall waiting for the lift-boy, who generally conducts strangers to the various floors. But this bright-eyed falcon of a girl had openly refused to endure such official delay. She said sharply that she knew all about the lift, and was not dependent on boys—or men either. Though her flat was only three floors above, she managed in the few seconds of ascent to give Flambeau a great many of her fundamental views in an off-hand manner; they were to the general effect that she was a modern working woman and loved modern working machinery. Her bright black eyes blazed with abstract anger against those who rebuke mechanic science and ask for the return of romance. Everyone, she said, ought to be able to manage machines, just as she could manage the lift. She seemed almost to resent the fact of Flambeau opening the lift-door for her; and that gentleman went up to his own apartments smiling

with somewhat
mingled feelings
at the memory
of such spit-fire
self-dependence.

She certainly had a
temper, of a snappy,
practical sort; the
gestures of her
thin, elegant hands
were abrupt or even
destructive.

Once Flambeau
entered her office
on some typewriting

business, and found
she had just flung
a pair of spectacles
belonging to her
sister into the middle
of the floor and
stamped on them.
She was already
in the rapids of an
ethical tirade about
the "sickly medical
notions" and the
morbid admission of
weakness implied in
such an apparatus.
She dared her

sister to bring such artificial, unhealthy rubbish into the place again. She asked if she was expected to wear wooden legs or false hair or glass eyes; and as she spoke her eyes sparkled like the terrible crystal.

Flambeau, quite bewildered with this fanaticism, could not refrain from asking Miss Pauline (with direct French logic) why a pair of spectacles was a more morbid sign of weakness than a lift, and why, if science might help us in the one effort, it might not help us in the other.

"That is so different," said Pauline Stacey, loftily. "Batteries and motors and all those things are marks of the force of man—yes, Mr. Flambeau, and the force of woman, too! We shall take our turn at these great engines that devour distance and defy time. That is high and splendid—that is really science. But these nasty props and plasters the doctors sell—why, they are just badges of poltroonery. Doctors stick on legs and arms as if we were born cripples and sick slaves. But I was free-born, Mr. Flambeau! People only think they need these things because they have been trained in fear instead of being trained in power and courage, just as the silly nurses tell children not to stare at the sun, and so they can't do it without blinking. But why among the stars should there be one star I may not see? The sun is not my master, and I will open my eyes and stare at him whenever I choose."

"Your eyes," said Flambeau, with a foreign bow, "will dazzle the sun."

He took pleasure in complimenting this strange stiff beauty, partly because it threw her a little off her balance. But as he went upstairs to his floor he drew a deep breath and whistled, saying to himself: "So she has got into the hands of that conjurer upstairs with his golden eye." For, little as he knew or cared about the new religion of Kalon, he had heard of his special notion about sun-gazing.

He soon discovered that the spiritual bond between the floors above and below him was close and increasing. The man who called himself Kalon was a magnificent creature, worthy, in a physical sense, to be the pontiff of Apollo. He was nearly as tall even as Flambeau, and very much better looking, with a golden beard, strong blue eyes, and a mane flung back like a lion's. In structure he was the blonde beast of Nietzsche, but all this animal beauty was heightened, brightened and softened by genuine intellect and spirituality. If he looked like one of the great Saxon kings, he looked like one of the kings that were also saints. And this despite the cockney incongruity of his surroundings; the fact that he had an office half-way up a building in Victoria Street; that the clerk (a commonplace youth in cuffs and collars) sat in the outer room, between him and the corridor; that his name was on a brass plate, and the gilt emblem of his creed hung above his street, like the advertisement of an oculist. All this vulgarity could not take away from the man called Kalon the vivid oppression and inspiration that came from his soul and body. When all was said, a man in the presence of this quack did feel in the presence of a great man. Even in the loose jacket-suit of linen that he wore as a workshop dress in his office he was a fascinating and formidable figure; and when robed in the white vestments and crowned with the golden circlet, in which he daily saluted the sun, he really looked so splendid that the laughter of the street people sometimes died suddenly on their lips. For three times in the day the new sun-worshipper went out on his little balcony, in the face of all Westminster, to say some litany to his shining lord: once at daybreak, once at sunset, and once at

the shock of noon.
And it was while
the shock of noon
still shook faintly
from the towers of
Parliament and parish
church that Father
Brown, the friend
of Flambeau, first
looked up and saw
the white priest of
Apollo.

Flambeau had
seen quite enough
of these daily

salutations of Phoebus, and plunged into the porch of the tall building without even looking for his clerical friend to follow. But Father Brown, whether from a professional interest in ritual or a strong individual interest in tomfoolery, stopped and stared up at the balcony of the sun-worshipper, just as he might have stopped and stared up at a Punch and Judy. Kalon the Prophet was already erect, with argent garments and uplifted hands, and the sound of his strangely penetrating voice could be heard all the way down the busy street uttering his solar litany. He was already in the middle of it; his eyes were fixed upon the flaming disc. It is doubtful if he saw anything or anyone on this earth; it is substantially certain that he did not see a stunted, round-faced priest who, in the crowd below, looked up at him with blinking eyes. That was perhaps the most startling difference between even these two far divided men. Father Brown could not look at anything without blinking; but the priest of Apollo could look on the blaze at noon without a quiver of the eyelid.

"O sun," cried the prophet, "O star that art too great to be allowed among the stars! O fountain that flowest quietly in that secret spot that is called space.

White Father of all white unwearied things, white flames and white flowers and white peaks. Father, who art more innocent than all thy most innocent and quiet children; primal purity, into the peace of which—"

A rush and crash like the reversed rush of a rocket was cloven with a strident and incessant yelling. Five people rushed into the gate of the mansions as three people rushed out, and for an instant they all deafened each other. The sense of some utterly abrupt horror seemed for a moment to fill half the street with bad news—bad news that was all the worse because no one knew what it was. Two figures remained still after the crash of commotion: the fair priest of Apollo on the balcony above, and the ugly priest of Christ below him.

At last the tall figure and titanic energy of Flambeau appeared in the doorway of the mansions and dominated the little mob. Talking at the

top of his voice
like a fog-horn, he
told somebody or
anybody to go for a
surgeon; and as he
turned back into the
dark and thronged
entrance his friend
Father Brown dipped
in insignificantly
after him. Even as
he ducked and dived
through the crowd he
could still hear the
magnificent melody
and monotony of

the solar priest still calling on the happy god who is the friend of fountains and flowers.

Father Brown found Flambeau and some six other people standing round the enclosed space into which the lift commonly descended. But the lift had not descended. Something else had descended; something that ought to have come by a lift.

For the last four minutes Flambeau had looked down on it; had seen the brained and bleeding figure of that beautiful woman who denied the existence of tragedy. He had never had the slightest doubt that it was Pauline Stacey; and, though he had sent for a doctor, he had not the slightest doubt that she was dead.

He could not remember for certain whether he had liked her or disliked her; there was so much both to like and dislike. But she had been a person to him, and the

unbearable pathos
of details and habit
stabbed him with all
the small daggers
of bereavement.
He remembered
her pretty face and
priggish speeches
with a sudden
secret vividness
which is all the
bitterness of death.
In an instant like a
bolt from the blue,
like a thunderbolt
from nowhere,

that beautiful and defiant body had been dashed down the open well of the lift to death at the bottom. Was it suicide? With so insolent an optimist it seemed impossible. Was it murder? But who was there in those hardly inhabited flats to murder anybody? In a rush of raucous words, which he meant to be strong and suddenly found weak, he asked where was that fellow Kalon. A voice, habitually heavy, quiet and full, assured him that Kalon for the last fifteen minutes had been away up on his balcony worshipping his god. When Flambeau heard the voice, and felt the hand of Father

Brown, he turned his swarthy face and said abruptly:

"Then, if he has been up there all the time, who can have done it?"

"Perhaps," said the other, "we might go upstairs and find out. We have half an hour before the police will move."

Leaving the body

of the slain heiress in charge of the surgeons, Flambeau dashed up the stairs to the typewriting office, found it utterly empty, and then dashed up to his own. Having entered that, he abruptly returned with a new and white face to his friend.

"Her sister," he said, with an unpleasant

seriousness, "her sister seems to have gone out for a walk."

Father Brown nodded. "Or, she may have gone up to the office of that sun man," he said. "If I were you I should just verify that, and then let us all talk it over in your office. No," he added suddenly, as if remembering something, "shall I ever get over that stupidity of mine? Of course, in their office downstairs."

Flambeau stared; but he followed the little father downstairs to the empty flat of the Staceys, where that impenetrable pastor took a large red-leather chair in the very entrance, from which he could see the stairs and landings, and waited. He did not wait very long. In about four minutes three figures descended the stairs, alike only in their solemnity. The first was Joan Stacey, the sister of the dead woman—evidently she had been upstairs in the temporary temple of Apollo; the second was the priest of Apollo himself, his litany finished, sweeping down the empty stairs in utter magnificence—something in his white robes, beard and parted hair had the look of Dore's Christ leaving the Pretorium; the third was Flambeau, black browed and somewhat bewildered.

Miss Joan Stacey, dark, with a drawn

face and hair prematurely touched with grey, walked straight to her own desk and set out her papers with a practical flap. The mere action rallied everyone else to sanity. If Miss Joan Stacey was a criminal, she was a cool one. Father Brown regarded her for some time with an odd little smile, and then, without taking his eyes off her, addressed himself to somebody else.

"Prophet," he said, presumably addressing Kalon, "I wish you would tell me a lot about your religion."

"I shall be proud to do it," said Kalon, inclining his still crowned head, "but I am not sure that I understand."

"Why, it's like this," said Father Brown, in his frankly doubtful way: "We are taught that if a man has really bad first principles, that must be partly his fault. But, for all that, we can make some difference between a man who insults his quite clear conscience and a man with a conscience more or less clouded with sophistries. Now, do you really think that murder is wrong at all?"

"Is this an accusation?" asked Kalon very quietly.

"No," answered Brown, equally gently, "it is the speech for the defence."

In the long and startled stillness of the room the prophet of Apollo slowly rose; and really it was like the rising of the sun. He filled that room with his light and life in such a manner that a man felt he could as easily have filled Salisbury Plain. His robed form seemed to hang the whole room with classic draperies; his epic

gesture seemed
to extend it into
grander perspectives,
till the little black
figure of the modern
cleric seemed to
be a fault and an
intrusion, a round,
black blot upon some
splendour of Hellas.

"We meet at last,
Caiaphas," said
the prophet. "Your
church and mine are
the only realities on

this earth. I adore the sun, and you the darkening of the sun; you are the priest of the dying and I of the living God. Your present work of suspicion and slander is worthy of your coat and creed. All your church is but a black police; you are only spies and detectives seeking to tear from men confessions of guilt, whether by treachery or torture. You would convict men of crime, I would convict them of innocence. You would convince them of sin, I would convince them of virtue.

"Reader of the books of evil, one more word before I blow away your baseless nightmares for ever. Not even faintly could you understand how little I care whether you can convict me or no. The things you call disgrace and horrible hanging are to me no more than an ogre in a child's toy-book to a man once grown up. You said you were offering the speech for the defence. I care so little for the cloudland of this life that I will offer you the speech for the prosecution. There is but one thing that can be said against me in this matter, and I will say it myself. The woman that is dead was my love and my bride; not after such manner as your tin chapels call lawful, but by a law purer and sterner than you will ever understand. She and I walked another world from yours, and trod palaces of crystal while you were plodding through tunnels and corridors of brick. Well, I know that policemen, theological and otherwise, always fancy that where there has been love there must soon be hatred; so there you have the first point made for the prosecution. But the second point is stronger; I do not grudge it you. Not only is it true that Pauline loved me, but it is also true that this very morning, before she died, she wrote at that table a will leaving me and my new church half a million. Come, where are the handcuffs? Do you suppose I care what foolish things you do with me? Penal servitude will only be like waiting for her at a wayside station. The gallows will only be going to her in a headlong car."

He spoke with the brain-shaking authority of an orator, and Flambeau and Joan Stacey stared at him in amazed admiration.

Father Brown's face seemed to express nothing but extreme distress; he looked at the ground with one wrinkle of pain across his forehead. The prophet of the sun leaned easily against the mantelpiece and resumed:

"In a few words I have put before you the whole case

against me—the only possible case against me. In fewer words still I will blow it to pieces, so that not a trace of it remains. As to whether I have committed this crime, the truth is in one sentence: I could not have committed this crime. Pauline Stacey fell from this floor to the ground at five minutes past twelve. A hundred people will go into the witness-box and say that I was standing out upon the balcony of my own rooms above from just before the stroke of noon to a quarter-past—the usual period of my public prayers. My clerk (a respectable youth from Clapham, with no sort of connection with me) will swear that he sat in my outer office all the morning, and that no communication passed through. He will swear that I arrived a full ten minutes before the hour, fifteen minutes before any whisper of the accident, and that I did not leave the office or the balcony all that time. No one ever had so complete an alibi; I could subpoena half

Westminster. I think you had better put the handcuffs away again. The case is at an end.

"But last of all, that no breath of this idiotic suspicion remain in the air, I will tell you all you want to know. I believe I do know how my unhappy friend came by her death. You can, if you choose, blame me for it, or my faith and philosophy at least; but you certainly cannot lock me up. It is well known to all students of the higher truths that certain adepts and illuminati have in history attained the power of levitation—that is, of being self-sustained upon the empty air. It is but a part of that

general conquest
of matter which is
the main element in
our occult wisdom.
Poor Pauline was
of an impulsive and
ambitious temper.
I think, to tell the
truth, she thought
herself somewhat
deeper in the
mysteries than she
was; and she has
often said to me,
as we went down
in the lift together,

that if one's will were strong enough, one could float down as harmlessly as a feather. I solemnly believe that in some ecstasy of noble thoughts she attempted the miracle. Her will, or faith, must have failed her at the crucial instant, and the lower law of matter had its horrible revenge.

There is the whole story, gentlemen, very sad and, as you think, very presumptuous and wicked, but certainly not criminal or in any way connected with me. In the short-hand of the police-courts, you had better call it suicide. I shall always call it heroic failure for the advance of science and the slow scaling of heaven."

It was the first time Flambeau had ever seen Father Brown vanquished. He still sat looking at the ground, with a painful and corrugated brow, as if in shame. It was impossible to avoid the feeling which the prophet's winged words had fanned, that here was a sullen, professional suspecter of men overwhelmed by a prouder and purer spirit of natural liberty and health. At last he said, blinking as if in bodily distress: "Well, if that is so, sir, you need do no more than take the testamentary paper you spoke of and go. I wonder where the poor lady left it."

"It will be over there on her desk by the

door, I think," said Kalon, with that massive innocence of manner that seemed to acquit him wholly. "She told me specially she would write it this morning, and I actually saw her writing as I went up in the lift to my own room."

"Was her door open then?" asked the priest, with his eye

on the corner of the matting.

"Yes," said Kalon calmly.

"Ah! it has been open ever since," said the other, and resumed his silent study of the mat.

"There is a paper over here," said the grim Miss Joan, in a somewhat singular voice. She had passed over to her sister's desk by the doorway, and was holding a sheet of blue foolscap in her hand. There was a sour smile on her face that seemed unfit for such a scene or occasion, and Flambeau looked at her with a darkening brow.

Kalon the prophet stood away from the

paper with that loyal unconsciousness that had carried him through. But Flambeau took it out of the lady's hand, and read it with the utmost amazement. It did, indeed, begin in the formal manner of a will, but after the words "I give and bequeath all of which I die possessed" the writing abruptly stopped with a set of scratches, and there was no trace of the name of any legatee. Flambeau, in wonder, handed this truncated testament to his clerical friend, who glanced at it and silently gave it to the priest of the sun.

An instant afterwards that pontiff, in his splendid sweeping draperies, had crossed the room in

two great strides,
and was towering
over Joan Stacey, his
blue eyes standing
from his head.

"What monkey
tricks have you been
playing here?" he
cried. "That's not all
Pauline wrote."

They were startled
to hear him speak
in quite a new
voice, with a Yankee
shrillness in it; all his

grandeur and good English had fallen from him like a cloak.

"That is the only thing on her desk," said Joan, and confronted him steadily with the same smile of evil favour.

Of a sudden the man broke out into blasphemies and cataracts of incredulous words.

There was something shocking about the dropping of his mask; it was like a man's real face falling off.

"See here!" he cried in broad American, when he was breathless with cursing, "I may be an adventurer, but I guess you're a murderess. Yes, gentlemen, here's your death explained, and without any levitation. The poor girl is writing a will in my favour; her cursed sister comes in, struggles for the pen, drags her to the well, and throws her down before she can finish it. Sakes! I reckon we want the handcuffs after all."

"As you have truly remarked," replied Joan, with ugly calm,

"your clerk is a very respectable young man, who knows the nature of an oath; and he will swear in any court that I was up in your office arranging some typewriting work for five minutes before and five minutes after my sister fell. Mr. Flambeau will tell you that he found me there."

There was a silence.

"Why, then," cried Flambeau, "Pauline was alone when she fell, and it was suicide!"

"She was alone when she fell," said Father Brown, "but it was not suicide."

"Then how did she die?" asked Flambeau impatiently.

"She was murdered."

"But she was alone," objected the detective.

"She was murdered when she was all alone," answered the priest.

All the rest stared at him, but he remained sitting in the same old dejected attitude, with a wrinkle in his round forehead and

an appearance of
impersonal shame
and sorrow; his voice
was colourless and
sad.

"What I want to
know," cried Kalon,
with an oath, "is
when the police
are coming for this
bloody and wicked
sister. She's killed
her flesh and blood;
she's robbed me of
half a million that

was just as sacredly mine as—"

"Come, come, prophet," interrupted Flambeau, with a kind of sneer; "remember that all this world is a cloudland."

The hierophant of the sun-god made an effort to climb back on his pedestal. "It is not the mere money," he cried, "though that would equip the cause throughout the world. It is also my beloved one's wishes. To Pauline all this was holy. In Pauline's eyes—"

Father Brown suddenly sprang erect, so that his chair fell over flat behind him. He was deathly pale, yet he seemed fired with a hope; his eyes shone.

"That's it!" he cried

in a clear voice. "That's the way to begin. In Pauline's eyes—"

The tall prophet retreated before the tiny priest in an almost mad disorder. "What do you mean? How dare you?" he cried repeatedly.

"In Pauline's eyes," repeated the priest, his own shining more and more. "Go on—in

God's name, go on. The foulest crime the fiends ever prompted feels lighter after confession; and I implore you to confess. Go on, go on—in Pauline's eyes—"

"Let me go, you devil!" thundered Kalon, struggling like a giant in bonds. "Who are you, you cursed spy, to weave your spiders' webs round me, and peep and peer? Let me go."

"Shall I stop him?" asked Flambeau, bounding towards the exit, for Kalon had already thrown the door wide open.

"No; let him pass," said Father Brown, with a strange deep sigh that seemed to come from the depths of the universe. "Let Cain pass by, for he belongs to God."

There was a long-drawn silence in the room when he had left it, which was to Flambeau's fierce wits one long agony of interrogation. Miss Joan Stacey very coolly tidied up the papers on her desk.

"Father," said

Flambeau at last, "it is my duty, not my curiosity only—it is my duty to find out, if I can, who committed the crime."

"Which crime?" asked Father Brown.

"The one we are dealing with, of course," replied his impatient friend.

"We are dealing

with two crimes,"
said Brown, "crimes
of very different
weight—and by very
different criminals."

Miss Joan Stacey,
having collected and
put away her papers,
proceeded to lock up
her drawer. Father
Brown went on,
noticing her as little
as she noticed him.

"The two crimes,"
he observed, "were

committed against the same weakness of the same person, in a struggle for her money. The author of the larger crime found himself thwarted by the smaller crime; the author of the smaller crime got the money."

"Oh, don't go on like a lecturer," groaned Flambeau; "put it in a few words."

"I can put it in one word," answered his friend.

Miss Joan Stacey skewered her business-like black hat on to her head with a business-like black frown before a little mirror, and, as the conversation proceeded, took her handbag and umbrella in an unhurried style, and left the room.

"The truth is one word, and a short one," said Father Brown. "Pauline Stacey was blind."

"Blind!" repeated Flambeau, and rose slowly to his whole huge stature.

"She was subject to it by blood," Brown proceeded. "Her sister would have

started eyeglasses
if Pauline would have
let her; but it was her
special philosophy
or fad that one must
not encourage such
diseases by yielding
to them. She would
not admit the cloud;
or she tried to dispel
it by will. So her
eyes got worse and
worse with straining;
but the worst strain
was to come. It came
with this precious

prophet, or whatever he calls himself, who taught her to stare at the hot sun with the naked eye. It was called accepting Apollo. Oh, if these new pagans would only be old pagans, they would be a little wiser! The old pagans knew that mere naked Nature-worship must have a cruel side. They knew that the eye of Apollo can blast and blind."

There was a pause, and the priest went on in a gentle and even broken voice. "Whether or no that devil deliberately made her blind, there is no doubt that he deliberately killed her through her blindness. The very simplicity of the crime is sickening. You know he and she went up and down in those lifts without official help; you know also how smoothly and silently the lifts slide. Kalon brought the lift to the girl's landing, and saw her, through the open door, writing in her slow, sightless way the will she had promised him. He called out to her cheerily that he had the lift ready for her, and she was to come out when she was ready. Then he pressed a button and shot soundlessly up to his own floor, walked through his own office, out on to his own balcony, and was safely praying before the crowded street when the poor girl, having finished her work, ran gaily out to where lover and lift were to receive her, and stepped—"

"Don't!" cried Flambeau.

"He ought to have got half a million by pressing that button," continued the little father, in the colourless voice in which he talked of such horrors. "But that went smash. It went smash because there happened to be another person who also wanted the money, and who also knew the secret about poor Pauline's sight. There was one thing about that will that I think nobody noticed: although it was unfinished and without signature, the other Miss Stacey and some servant of hers had already signed it as witnesses. Joan had signed first, saying Pauline could finish it later, with a typical feminine contempt for legal forms. Therefore, Joan wanted her sister to sign the will without real witnesses. Why? I thought of the blindness, and felt sure she had wanted Pauline to sign in solitude because she had wanted her not to sign at all.

"People like the Staceys always use fountain pens; but this was specially natural to Pauline. By habit and her strong will and memory she could still write almost as well as if she saw; but she could not tell when her pen needed dipping. Therefore, her fountain pens were carefully filled by her sister—all except this fountain pen. This was carefully not filled by her sister; the remains of the ink held out for a few lines and then failed altogether. And the prophet lost five hundred thousand pounds and committed one of the most brutal and brilliant murders in human history for nothing."

Flambeau went to the open door and heard the official police ascending the stairs. He turned and said: "You must have followed everything devilish close to have traced the crime to Kalon in ten minutes."

Father Brown gave a sort of start.

"Oh! to him," he said. "No; I had to follow

rather close to find out about Miss Joan and the fountain pen. But I knew Kalon was the criminal before I came into the front door."

"You must be joking!" cried Flambeau.

"I'm quite serious," answered the priest. "I tell you I knew he had done it, even before I knew what he had done."

"But why?"

"These pagan stoics," said Brown reflectively, "always fail by their strength. There came a crash and a scream down the street, and the priest of Apollo did not start or look round. I did not know what it was. But I knew that he was expecting it."

ABOUT THE AUTHOR

G.K. Chesteron was an English writer, poet, philosopher, journalist, orator, lay theologian, biographer, and critic. He wrote around 80 books, several hundred poems, some 200 short stories, 4000 essays, and several plays. He had a tendency to forget where he was supposed to be going and miss the train that was supposed to take him there. It is reported that on several occasions he sent a telegram to his wife Frances from some distant (and incorrect) location, writing such things as "Am in Market Harborough. Where ought I to be?" to which she would reply, "Home".

WHAT WE'RE ABOUT

I started making Super Large Print books for my grandma. I wanted books that she could keep reading as her glaucoma and macular degeneration advanced. So I chose a font originally designed for people with dyslexia, because the letters are bold and easy to distinguish. It is set at 30 pt, nearly twice the size of traditional Large Print books.

Digital reading was too frustrating for my grandma. It could never offer the pleasures she had always associated with reading: the peacefulness of turning a page, the satisfaction in knowing a story has "this much left," and the comforting memories of adventure, companionship, and revelation she felt when seeing the cover of her favorite book. Part of what makes reading so relaxing and grounding is the tactile experience. I hope these books can bring joy to those who want to keep reading and to those who've never had the pleasure of curling up with a page turner.

Please let me know if these books are helpful to you and if you have any requests for new titles. To leave feedback and to see the complete and constantly updating catalog, please visit:

superlargeprint.com

MORE BOOKS AT:

superlargeprint.com

KEEP ON READING!

This book is set in a font designed by Abelardo Gonzalez called OpenDyslexic

ISBN 9781086232189

Printed in Great Britain
by Amazon

56262373R00076